PROTECTING LILA

SEAL TEAM ALPHA
BOOK 1

SHAW HART

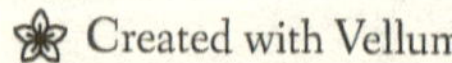 Created with Vellum

WANT A FREE BOOK?

You can grab Sweets Here.
**Check out my website, www.shawhart.com for
more free books!**

This grumpy SEAL might have just met his match...

Lila

When Warren moves in next door to me, I'm instantly drawn to the scarred giant.

I know right away that he's meant to be mine.

Too bad for me, he's playing hard to get.

Warren

I don't want to be back in California.

I didn't want this assignment.

It feels like I'm being sidelined.

The only bright spot in my days has been my curvy new neighbor.

I'm determined not to put down roots here, but something deep down inside of me is telling me that she's the one for me.

When I get the offer to go back to active duty, will I choose to stay with my sweet sunshine or go back to where I always thought I wanted to be?

ONE

Warren

I DON'T WANT *to be here.*

That's all I can think as I grab another box from the back of my truck and turn to bring it up to my new apartment. I don't want to be here; I don't want to be doing this, but I don't have a choice.

"You should try not to look so miserable. You're moving into a new apartment, not storming an enemy camp," my friend and fellow Navy SEAL, Keaton, tells me as he follows me into my new apartment with another one of my boxes.

The truth is, I'd much rather be overseas, getting shot at and risking my life than being here.

"Would you be happy about this?" I ask, motioning around to the empty apartment.

California is crazy expensive, and housing on base was all full, so I'm in a single-bedroom apartment a few miles from the base and the beach. The place is kind of run-down, but it was the cleanest and nicest apartment I could find, especially on such short notice.

"It's fine. It has a fridge and a bed," Keaton grunts, and I try to hide my smile.

Keaton is pretty simple. As long as he has somewhere to sleep and put his food, he's good. Being deployed so many times will do that to you. You get used to being happy with just the necessities.

It was right after my last deployment that I was told about this new assignment. When I had been called into my Commander's office and told that I was being sent back to Coronado, I had tried to get out of it, to get picked for literally any other assignment, but it was no use.

I know that they were worried about me after my last deployment. We were ambushed my last month there and lost quite a few of our guys, people that I had deployed with before and been close to. I know I probably needed a break, but this wasn't what I had in mind.

I've been in the Navy for six years and deployed four times. I've grown used to being on high alert and always being aware of my surroundings. Now, I'm going to be teaching others how to prepare for that.

"I guess," I tell Keaton as we set our boxes down and look around the place.

"Maybe paint," he suggests, and I glare at him.

"I'm not going to be here long enough for that to matter."

"You might be," he points out, and I glare at him.

"I won't," I assure him, but deep down, I know that that's not entirely true.

I might be here for a few months, or it could be years. I shudder at that thought.

"Shouldn't you be going? You don't want to miss your father's funeral," I grunt at Keaton, and he glares at me.

Keaton is on bereavement leave. He's supposed to be attending his father's funeral and taking a few weeks off to grieve. The truth is that Keaton's father was a real prick, and he won't be missed by anyone, least of all his son. Keaton has told me a few stories about him over the years, and I don't blame him one bit for skipping the funeral. I would do the same thing if I were in his shoes.

"What are you two bickering about now?" Anson asks as he and the other guys come into my new apartment.

"Nothing," Keaton and I answer at the same time.

Anson, Rhett, Kye, and Gates were all in the SEALs with us, though they got out about a year ago and opened their own security company here in Los Angeles. They asked Keaton and I to join them, but we both wanted to stay in. Now that I'm here, teaching at Coronado, I'm wondering if I should have taken them up on their offer.

Gates sets the last of the boxes down on the stack, and I glare at the box. I told my friends they didn't have to help me move in. It's not like I have a lot of stuff to unpack anyway, but they insisted. I think they're just hoping that I offer to buy them some pizza and beer.

"You could make this move permanent and join us at Knight Security," Rhett says with an easy grin, and I shake my head.

He's always been the most laid-back of all of us. Even getting shot overseas didn't dim his outlook on life.

Maybe I should be more like that. Try to look at the positives of this new job. Maybe I'll find a woman like all my friends did and want to settle down here.

Somehow, I can't bring myself to believe that. I've never been interested all that much in the opposite sex. I always thought that maybe there was something wrong with me. None of my friends ever cared about women either, but then they met their wives and BAM! That was it for them.

"No thanks," I tell Rhett, turning down his job offer.

I've always loved serving my country. It's why I joined the military as soon as I graduated high school. It's why I worked hard to become a SEAL. I wanted to be useful, to prove my worth. Being here, though, teaching doesn't feel like I'm doing that, though.

"Maybe you'll love teaching," Keaton suggests, and I give him a dry look.

"Maybe," I say, but I don't sound very convincing.

"Well, why don't you buy us a beer, and we can catch up?" Kye suggests, and I bite back a grin.

"I knew that was why you all offered to help me move in," I say with a laugh and they smirk.

"Guilty. Come on now, I'm thirsty," Anson complains, and we all file out of the apartment.

They start to head down the stairs towards the parking lot while I stop to lock the door. I'm determined not to think about starting at Coronado tomorrow and just focus on having fun with my friends.

I lock the door and pocket my keys when the door next to mine opens, and the most beautiful woman I've ever seen walks out. Her shoulder-length dark brown hair is half pulled up into a bun on top of her head. Loose strands fall around her face, obscuring my view, but even without seeing her face, something about her calls to me. There's a twisting in my chest when I look at her, and I swallow hard as she turns to face me.

Her blue eyes twinkle as she smiles at me. She's so pretty, so full of optimism and life.

She's carrying a trash bag, and my first instinct is to

reach out and take it. I don't realize that I've actually done that until she blinks her big blue eyes up at me.

"Oh," she says in surprise, staring at my hand that's now tightly gripping the garbage bag.

"I'm headed down. I'll take this for you," I grit out.

"Um, thanks," she says with a wide, friendly smile.

"Not a problem," I grunt, and my hand tightens even more around the garbage bag.

I have the strangest desire to reach out and touch her, but I know I can't do that.

Keep it together, Warren.

Is this what it felt like for my friends? Is this how it was when they all met their wives? "Did you just move in?" She asks, and I nod. "Well, welcome to Paradise Cove."

I didn't think that this place was much of a paradise. I had even scoffed when I saw the apartment building's name. Now, though, I'm starting to see the appeal of this place.

"Thanks."

"I'm Lila, by the way."

"Warren," I say gruffly, and she smiles.

"I'll see you around, neighbor," my girl says as she waves and turns to head back into her apartment.

"See you, sunshine," I murmur as I stare after her.

I watch her curvy ass as she walks away, and my cock hardens in my jeans at the sight. I've never really noticed women before, but there's something about Lila that calls to me. I want her. I want to get to know her. I want to make her smile at me again. I want to know everything that there is to know about her. I want to take care of her.

Suddenly, being here and having to teach at Coronado is looking a whole hell of a lot better.

I jog down the stairs and toss the garbage in the dumpster as I head over to my truck. Keaton is already inside, and he raises an eyebrow at me.

"Who was that?"

"Her name's Lila. She's my new neighbor."

"Looked like you wanted her to be a heck of a lot more than that," he says, giving me a knowing smirk, and I stiffen.

Do I really want to start something with my new neighbor? My cock says yes, but I need to think about this clearly. I don't want to put down roots here. I want to do my time and then return to being deployed and in the action, not teaching people about it.

"I don't," I lie to Keaton, and he shakes his head at me, clearly not believing a word I said.

I ignore him as I lead us over to my truck and climb in.

I need to stay away and keep my eyes on the game plan, I think as I start my truck and follow Anson's car out onto the road. I can't help but look in the rearview mirror at my new neighbor's door as I go though.

TWO

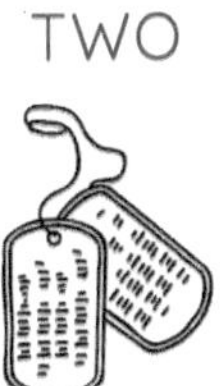

Lila

I SHOULD BE WORKING, but I find myself over by the front window of my apartment, staring out at the parking lot for any sign of my new neighbor's truck. He's been gone all day. I would know. I've spent most of the day looking for any sign of him.

I haven't seen him in a few days. Not since he moved in. He must wake up crazy early because I'm usually up before eight, and every single day, he's already left.

My phone rings, and I pull it out of my pocket, already knowing it's my best friend, Pia, who's calling me.

"Hey, how's it going?" I answer.

"Slow. I'm making dinner and waiting for Levi to get home from work."

"What are you making?"

"Tacos."

"Good choice," I say, and I know that she's smiling.

"What about you? How are you feeling?" She asks me.

"Good. A little tired, but good."

"When's your next doctor's appointment?"

"I have a checkup in two weeks."

Pia lets out a breath and I know she's worried about me. I had pancreatic cancer, but after my surgery a few months ago, I've been in remission. Still, I know that both of us are worried about the cancer coming back.

"How's Levi?" I ask.

I know that Pia will be distracted by thoughts of her new husband, and the conversation can move onto more positive topics. Levi and Pia just got married recently. She was working for him, trying to make money to pay for my surgery. They ended up falling in love, and he was generous enough to cover my surgery and all of the doctor's appointments that went along with that.

They wanted me to move in with them, but I knew they needed their privacy and alone time. When I turned that offer down, they offered to buy me a place near theirs, but they have already done so much for me. I didn't want to take advantage of them. I want to stand on my own two feet.

Levi worships the ground that Pia walks on. He was hooked from the first moment he saw her, and their romance was a bit of a whirlwind. Pia has been taking care of me for far too long, so it's nice to see her being taken care of for a change.

I started back at work after recovering from the surgery and moved into this little apartment when Pia moved into Levi's penthouse apartment. I work as a freelance social media manager and content creator. I've got a few bigger clients, and things have been great these past few months.

"What about you? How's your new neighbor?" She asks in a knowing tone. "Are you spying out the window right now?"

"Maybe," I admit, and she laughs.

"Any sign of him?"

"Not yet," I sigh, letting the blinds fall closed.

"Bummer. What are you going to do tonight? Want to come over for dinner?" She offers.

"No, I found a new recipe for some chicken kabobs. I'm going to try to make that tonight."

"Ohhh, sounds good! Let me know how they turn out."

"I will."

"Levi just got home, but I'll talk to you later. We'll grab lunch this week, yeah?"

"Sounds good. Just let me know when."

"I'll text you."

"Talk to you later."

"See you!" She says, and we end the call.

I want what Pia and Levi have. I want someone who loves me unconditionally. Someone who always supports me and is lifting me up. Someone who always has my back.

I've never been into dating. I never really had crushes on anyone, either. At first, it was because Pia and I were trying to work and support ourselves, and then I was diagnosed with cancer. I was starting to think that maybe I would never find anyone that sparked an interest in me. That was until the other day when I met Warren.

I know that he has to be the one for me. No one else has given me butterflies in my stomach. I can't get him off of my mind, and I'm taking that as a sign that he's meant to be mine. I just wonder if he feels any connection between us, too.

I blow out a deep breath and head towards the kitchen. I actually really love to cook now that I have an appetite again. I've been enjoying trying out new recipes and learning more about what spices I like and don't like.

I take out the chicken and focus on the recipe as I start to make dinner. I finish cutting up the chicken and putting them on the skewers. I'm a little nervous about over or undercooking the chicken as I start my countertop grill and turn it on to the correct heat. I know I'm not the best cook yet, but it should be fine.

Turns out it's not.

THREE

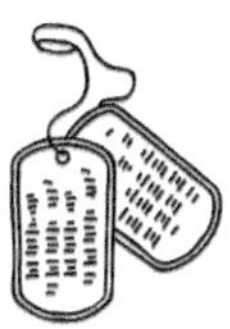

Warren

I'M exhausted when I get back to the apartment building. As soon as I park and climb out of my truck, my eyes go up to Lila's door, just like every other time I come home. This time, though, my eyes widen, and I take off when I see the smoke coming out of the front window of her place.

"Lila!" I shout as I take the stairs two at a time and burst into her apartment.

She's coughing, waving a kitchen towel around her kitchen to try to clear out the smoke. The smoke has the whole room looking hazy, but luckily for me, Lila is wearing a bright pink shirt and I focus on that color as I head her way.

"Oh, hey, Warren," Lila says like this is a completely normal occurrence.

"What happened? You need to get out of here," I say, already making my way towards her.

I grab her hand and tug her out the front door.

Touching her feels so right, so natural, but then I remember that I'm not getting attached to this place, and I release my hold on her like I've been burned.

"What happened?" I ask her again.

"I was making dinner," she says calmly.

"I think it was done... like five minutes ago."

"Yeah, it was a new recipe. I think I might have messed up a step or two."

"You need to be more careful."

"It's fine. I just need to open a few windows."

I sigh and head back into her apartment to start opening the other windows. She did the front room, which is why I saw the smoke, but we need to open more.

I head into the kitchen and look at the tiny burnt pieces of what I'm guessing was chicken. Lila is back to waving a dish towel around to blow the smoke out, and I lean back against the counter.

"So... how's work been? Are you enjoying California?" She asks, trying to make small talk.

I huff out a breath and cross my arms over my chest.

"Work has been busy. California is hot."

"Well, at least you're staying positive about the move," she comments.

I laugh, surprising both of us. The truth is that I have been focusing on the negatives. I don't want to get used to being here.

"Have you eaten yet? I'm going to order something if you want to join me."

"What are you having?" I ask before I can stop myself.

"How does pizza sound?"

"Sure."

I know I shouldn't agree, that I'm already too interested in this girl, but I can't hold myself back any longer. I've been thinking about Lila way too much. She pops into my head at the strangest times. I'm in the pool, supervising a group, and I picture Lila swimming next to me. I'm running alongside the guys, and wonder what she's doing right now. I even dream about her. Every night since I moved in.

"Is pepperoni okay?" Lila asks me, and I nod.

She's already ordering the food, so I take a moment to look around her apartment. The layout is the same as mine, with the living room up front and the kitchen in the back. Her hallway goes to the right, and I know that our bedrooms must butt up against each other through the wall.

An image of Lila, half naked and tangled in my sheets, flashes behind my eyes, and I clear my throat, shifting on my feet to try to hide my erection.

"Thirty minutes," Lila says, tucking her phone back into her pocket.

"I'm going to head home and shower, get changed and all that."

"Sounds good. I'll be here when you're done."

I force myself to turn and leave her apartment and head into my own place. It's bare and cold feeling compared to Lila's. I head into my room, pull off my uniform, and toss it in the hamper. I need to do laundry soon, but I'm too tired to do it tonight.

I shower and pull on a clean t-shirt and a pair of black sweatpants. It only took me twelve minutes to shower and change, but I still head back over to Lila's. She opens the door for me with a smile and my heart takes off like a shot.

Fuck. What this girl does to me...

"Pizza should be here soon," she tells me as I walk into her apartment.

"Okay."

"So, how are you liking California now that you've been here a few days?"

"It's okay. I like the weather," I say.

"Yeah, it's been nice out lately."

"Are you from California?"

"Yep, born and raised."

"Did you ever want to leave and go somewhere else?"

"No, I like it here. Well, besides the high prices and traffic," she says with a laugh. "My best friend, Pia, lives here, and I don't want to leave her. She's like a sister to me."

"I get that."

"What about you? You must have lived all over, being in the Navy."

"Yeah, I've been on the East Coast for the most part, with a few deployments."

"What was your favorite place?" She asks as we take a seat on the couch.

I pause, contemplating her question. Where was the last place that felt like home? When was the last time that I was happy?

"I'm not sure. A lot of these beachside bases all seem the same."

Her smile dims, and I try to think of something to say to bring it back.

"What do you do for a living?" I ask her.

"I'm a social media manager."

"That sounds cool."

"Yeah, I like it. I'm freelance, so I get to make my own schedule and set my own hours. Plus, I get to work from home, so I don't have to mess with the traffic."

I love how positive she always is. She's always looking on the bright side.

A knock sounds on the door, and she stands to answer it.

"Here, let me pay for it," I say, joining her at the door.

"Oh, it's okay. It will be my welcome to the neighborhood gift to you," she says with a sweet smile.

She passes me the pizza box and hands a twenty to the delivery driver.

"Thanks," she tells him, and he nods as he heads off.

"We can eat in the kitchen," she says, leading me to the back of the apartment.

"I like your apartment. It's a lot more welcoming than my place."

"Well, you just moved in. You have time to make it your own."

We each grab a slice and sit down at her little kitchen table to eat.

"It's good," I say, and she nods.

"Best pizza place in Los Angeles!" She agrees.

We both dig in, and she moans slightly as she takes a bite. My cock hardens, and all I can think about is pushing her up against the nearest surface and kissing her.

She's so sweet and optimistic, and I crave that. I want more of that in my life.

I clear my throat, trying to focus on my pizza instead of all of the things that I want to do to my sweet neighbor.

We make small talk as we eat. She tells me about some of her favorite places nearby and gives me tips on some good restaurants that are close by. I make note of the tips and debate asking her to join me for dinner soon.

Don't get attached. I'm not putting down roots, I remind myself.

"Thanks for dinner. I should be getting out of your hair," I say once we're done eating.

We both stand, and she smiles as she walks me to the

front door. I turn to say goodbye to her and freeze when I realize how close we are to each other.

My eyes drop to her lips, and I find myself leaning closer to her. Her eyelids flutter, and she licks her lips as her eyes drop to my mouth.

Her warm breath fans over my face, and I swallow hard. I can practically feel her lips under mine. I want to kiss her, know what she tastes like, and hear how she'll respond to me. I want it more than anything I've ever wanted before.

Roots, I think.

I snap out of the trance and clear my throat as I back up.

"Thanks again for dinner," I say in a rush before I head out the door.

I force myself to walk next door to my apartment and not look back at her. I unlock my apartment and head inside, leaning back against the door as I try to calm my racing heart.

That was a close one, I think. *I almost kissed her, and I know that if I had, I wouldn't have wanted to ever stop. I can't be stupid and act on my feelings here.*

I know that I did the right thing, or at least, I think that I did.

It doesn't feel right, though. It feels like I just made the big mistake of my life.

FOUR

Lila

I DON'T KNOW what's going on between Warren and me, but I'm determined to find out. I've been trying to catch him when he leaves for work or comes back, but I think he might be avoiding me after our almost kiss the other day.

I haven't seen him once since we ate dinner together, and each day that passes, I get a little more annoyed. I know that he has to be able to feel this thing between us, so why is he fighting it so much?

I don't have time to wait for him tonight. I'm meeting Pia at our favorite Asian fusion restaurant downtown, and I need to leave soon if I want to make it there on time.

I take a step back, admiring the deep red color of my dress. I just bought it the other day and I've been dying for an opportunity to wear it out. It's a little fancier than what I normally wear, but I love the color and the cut. The fabric hugs my curves and makes me feel sexy.

I wonder if Warren would like it.

I shut that thought down and grab my purse, making sure that I have my keys and my phone as I head for the door. I lock up my apartment and send a quick text to Pia, letting her know that I'm on my way.

Then I run right into a brick wall.

"Oomph!" I grunt, my hands shooting out to try to brace against something as I stumble back.

"I've got you, sunshine," Warren says, and I look up into his handsome face.

He looks tired today. Tired and pissed.

"Where are you going?" He demands to know, and I grind my teeth together.

He's been avoiding me all week, yet he wants to know what's new with me.

"Out to dinner," I tell him, and his eyes narrow.

He looks up and down my body, and I can tell that he likes what he sees. I can also tell that he's jealous and thinks I'm going out on a date.

"Who's the lucky guy?" He grits out, and I smile slightly.

"Wish I could stay and chat, but I'm running late. I'll see you later, neighbor."

I see his jaw flex as I start to walk past him, and then he's falling into step beside me.

"I'll walk you to your car."

"You don't have to."

"I shouldn't. You know, a real date would pick you up."

"Is that what you would do?" I ask him, and his mouth snaps shut.

"I don't date."

We reach my car, and I unlock it. He reaches for the door and opens it for me, surprising both of us.

"Uh, thanks."

He nods, his features tight, and I nod back. We're silent as I slide into the driver's seat and buckle up. Then he's leaning down so that we're eye to eye.

"Why don't you let me drive you?"

"I'm good. I know that you must be tired."

"I don't mind."

"Really, it's okay."

I can see that he wants to argue with me some more, but he bites his tongue and nods once.

"Be safe. Call me if you need anything."

"I don't have your number," I point out, and he pulls out his phone and passes it to me.

I enter my number, looking up at him with a frown when I pass the phone back to him. He calls me and hangs up once my phone rings.

"Now you do."

"Yeah."

Yeah, now you do.

How come he's been avoiding me all week? Then, as soon as he thinks I'm going out with someone else, he's all over me.

I was going to tell him that I was just seeing Pia for dinner, but now I'm too pissed off at him to bother to correct his assumptions.

"See you later."

I reach past him and grab the door handle, pulling the door closed. He has to jump out of the way, and I don't bother to look at him as I start the car and back out of my parking spot.

Part of me loves that he's finally showing some interest in me, but I shouldn't have to be going out with someone else for him to make a move. If he really wanted me, he should be man enough to tell me so.

I stew the entire drive to The Social Kitchen. When I park, Pia is already there and waiting for me by the front doors.

"Hey!" I greet her, running over to give her a hug.

It's still weird to not be living with her. We talk every day and try to meet up at least twice a week, but it's not the same as living together and getting to see her all the time.

"How's Levi?"

"He's good. He wanted me to tell you hi."

"Say hi back."

"I will. Come on, let's eat."

She loops her arm through mine, and I grin as we head inside. We get seated at a table in the back, and neither of us bothers with a menu. We get the same thing every time we come here.

"You look amazing, by the way. I love the dress! Is it new?"

"Yeah, I saw it in a store downtown. I had to take my car for an oil change and went window shopping while waiting."

"I love it. You'll have to let me borrow it sometime."

"Of course. My closet is your closet," I say with a laugh.

It's always been that way between us. We shared everything. It's kind of nice to see that not everything has changed.

The waiter comes by, and we both order; then she leans back and smiles at me.

"So... how's your new neighbor?"

"I don't know," I admit with a sigh. "He's confusing."

"How so?"

"We had dinner the other night," I say, and she nods.

She already knows all about our little kind of date the other night. She's been waiting for what she's been calling her "Warren updates" every day since. Unfortunately for both of us, I haven't had anything else to report.

"And then nothing. I haven't seen him since. I think he was avoiding me, but I ran into him tonight when I was leaving to come here."

"And?"

"I don't know, it was weird."

"Why?"

"He thinks that I'm on a date."

She blinks at me, and I grab my glass of water and take a sip.

"You told him that you were going on a date?" She asks, and I shake my head.

"No, he just assumed."

"Well, you do look hot."

I laugh, and she grins.

"And you didn't correct him?"

"No," I admit. "I was going to, but then I just got so mad. Like he doesn't want me, but he doesn't want anyone else to have me either."

"Oh, I think he wants you," she says slyly, and I shake my head.

"No. If he did, he wouldn't be avoiding me."

"What did he do when you were leaving?"

Our waiter drops off our edamame and I grab one.

"Well, he walked me to my car and told me how a real date would have come to pick me up."

"That's true," Pia agrees, and I roll my eyes.

"I asked him if that's what he would do, and he told me that he doesn't date."

"Maybe not before, but it sounds like he's warming up to the idea," she says with a smirk

"He opened my car door for me," I continue, and she nods. "Then he offered to drive me."

Pia snorts, and I try to hide my smile.

"Then what?" She asks.

"Um, he told me to call him if I needed anything, and I was like, I don't have your phone number, and he just handed me his phone."

"Has he texted or called you yet?"

"I don't know. I was driving, so I didn't look."

"Well, look now!" She tells me as the rest of our food is dropped off.

I grab another edamame and then pull my phone out.

"He did!" She cries with glee, and I grin.

"Yeah, he did."

I scan over the texts and by the end, I'm practically beaming.

WARREN: **Text me when you get to the restaurant.**

Warren: You don't owe him anything.

Warren: If he does anything to make you uncomfortable, you need to leave. You can call me and I'll come get you.

Warren: What restaurant are you at?

Warren: Sunshine, I'm starting to worry.

I SHOW PIA, and she practically melts at his texts.

"Aww, I wish Levi was like that," she sighs.

"Like what?" Her husband asks as he slides into the booth next to her.

"Warren is worried about Lila. He keeps checking in on her."

"I've texted you five times since you got here," Levi says with a smile.

"You have?" Pia asks, pulling out his phone.

"Yeah. When you didn't respond, I decided to come and check on you two."

"Oh, sorry, honey. I didn't hear it."

"I figured. Had to be sure, though."

Levi smiles at Pia like she's his entire world. That's what I want. I want someone to check in on me, someone who cares about my well-being and how I am. Someone who is crazy in love with me.

"What's new with you two?" I ask, changing the subject.

Pia shoots me a look, letting me know that she's not done talking about Warren, and I know that she'll bring him back up soon.

"Nothing much. We were talking about getting away for a few days soon. Want to come on vacation with us?" Levi asks, and I smile.

He's always been so welcoming and kind to me. I appreciate that. I know that he just wants Pia to be happy and that he knows that I love her as much as he does.

"Depends. Where are we going?"

I eat and listen to them debate the pros and cons of a few different places. I doubt that I'll go with them. I know they're still in the honeymoon phase, and I'm sure they don't want me third-wheeling their vacation.

I ask Levi about work as we finish eating, and he pays the bills.

"It's been good. Busy, but good."

He smiles at Pia, and my heart thumps hard in my chest.

Why couldn't Warren look at me like that?

My phone buzzes, and I glance down to see another message from Warren.

WARREN: **I'm losing my mind here, sunshine.**

SHOOT! *I forgot to text him back earlier.*

LILA: **I'm fine.**

Warren: That's it?

Warren: You're fine?

Warren: I've been freaking out for an hour and a half now.

Lila: You didn't have to. I'm okay.

THREE LITTLE DOTS appear on the screen, then disappear, then reappear, and I bite my bottom lip, waiting to see what he'll say, but they disappear again and stay gone.

I sigh, tucking my phone back into my purse as the waiter comes back and we get ready to leave.

"Sorry for crashing your date," Levi apologizes to us, but I wave him off.

"You're always welcome," I promise him.

He smiles as he offers Pia his hand and pulls her out of the booth.

"Want us to give you a ride home?" He offers, but I shake my head, holding up my keys.

"I drove. I'll be fine."

"I'll talk to you tomorrow," Pia promises me, and I know we'll be revisiting the Warren stuff.

"Sounds good. Good night, you two!"

I wave as I head over to my car, and they slip into the backseat of their SUV. Their driver waves at me as he passes, and I smile, pulling out after them and heading in the opposite direction.

I try not to think about Warren as I drive home, but I can't seem to help it. The one question that keeps circling around in my head is: *I wonder if he's done avoiding me yet?*

FIVE

Warren

"SHE'S STILL NOT BACK," I tell Keaton as I pace back and forth in the front room of my apartment.

"Well, did you tell her what her curfew was?" He asks, and I growl.

I hear him laugh, and I want to hang up on him, but he's the only one to answer my call, and I need him right now.

"Relax, Warren. It's a date," he points out, and I know that he's taking way too much enjoyment out of rubbing that in.

"Not helping."

"Calm down. Traffic in Los Angeles is crazy, right?"

"Yeah, it's a pain in the ass."

"Well, she's probably just stuck in traffic then."

"I guess," I grumble, my eyes trained on the dark parking lot.

"She should have been home by now. It's dark out. She's been gone for hours."

"Must have been a good date," Keaton muses, and I want to punch him in the face.

"I hate you."

"I miss you too."

"How's the East Coast?"

Silence greets me, and I wonder what could be going on with him.

"Uh, it's good," he says, but he sounds off.

"What are you not telling me?" I ask.

"Nothing," he says too quickly, and I wonder if maybe he's having lady trouble too.

Before I can ask, a pair of headlights turns into the parking lot, and I'm on high alert.

"She's home. I've got to go. I'll talk to you later."

"Later," he grunts, and we both hang out.

I rush out of my apartment and stop to see if it's Lila's car or not. That's when I see the hooded figure at the edge of the parking lot. It's obviously a man, judging by his build, and I know that he must be looking for Lila. She's the only one out here at this time of night.

I take the stairs two at a time down to the parking lot and over to Lila's car. My eyes stay glued to the hooded man, and he takes off when I get close to Lila.

I glance at her, and she's busy gathering her things. She has no idea that some man could have just attacked her, and I grit my teeth as I knock on the window. She jumps, yelping as she turns to face me.

That does it. This girl needs someone to protect her and look after her. I mean, she has no tactical awareness. If I was able to sneak up on her and I wasn't even trying, then I shudder to think what would have happened to her if it was someone else coming after her.

"You scared me," she says as she opens the door.

"You scared me. I thought something bad had happened to you on your date."

"I texted you that I was fine," she reminds me, and I growl.

"Yeah, hours later."

"I didn't see it until then."

She climbs out of the car and I look her over for any sign that she's been harmed. Her dress is still in place with no rips or tears, and she doesn't look like she's been crying or anything. I'm glad she's not hurt, but that means she had a good time on her date, and I hate that thought too.

"How was dinner?" I ask her, trying to keep my voice even.

"It was really good," she says with a wide smile, and I want to strangle the man that she was with.

"I'm surprised you didn't bring your date home then," I comment.

"Do you think that I should have?" She asks me.

"Fuck no," I snap.

She grins up at me, taking a step closer as I close her car door for her.

"What would you have done?" She asks me as she takes another step closer to me.

"What do you mean?"

"What would you have done if I was out with you?"

My stomach drops and I can't take it anymore. I want her; I have since the very first moment that I saw her, and I can't resist her any longer.

I step towards her, closing the gap between us. I reach up, cupping her face in my hands as I lower my mouth slowly to hers. Our eyes lock, and we watch each other as my mouth lands on hers. Her eyes flutter closed, and mine close soon after.

Her lips are so soft and full as they move against mine. She melts against me, and I bite back a groan as my hands drop to her waist and I pull her flush against me. Her curves fit perfectly against mine, and she moans as my erection digs into her soft stomach.

That has my blood heating, and I deepen the kiss. I lick against the seam of her lips, and she opens for me, just as greedy for me as I am for her.

My tongue slips into her mouth, and now it's my turn to moan. She tastes like sugar and honey. She tastes just as sweet as she is.

My fingers dig into her hips when she starts to squirm against me, and all I can think about is taking her to bed. Hell, I don't even need a bed. Her car is closer.

A car horn starts to beep nearby, and Lila gasps and pulls away from me. My hands cling to her for a moment before I reluctantly let her go.

Her eyes are wide and we stare at each other for a beat. All I can wonder is what happens now that I've opened that door between us because I don't want to close it.

Ever.

SIX

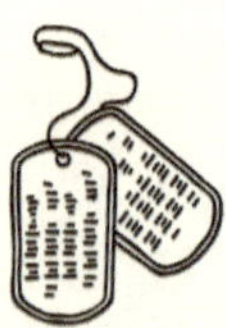

Lila

WARREN RELEASES ME, and I drop back down onto my heels. My lips are tingling from the way that he kissed me, and I can't help but grin up at him.

"It's about time," I tell him, and he laughs.

"I've wanted to do that since I met you," he admits.

"Why'd you wait so long?"

"It's... complicated."

I want to ask him more about that, but before I can, he's turning and motioning for me to walk with him. We head towards the stairs, and I reach out, taking his hand.

"Did your date kiss you?" He asks me suddenly, and I shake my head.

"I was out with Pia and her husband for dinner. It wasn't a date," I admit to him.

He blinks, looking shocked, and then he drops my hand like I've burned him. I can tell that he doesn't know how to feel about my little deception and I start to feel kind of guilty. Until he moves, stepping away from me and towards his apartment.

I frown, wanting to follow after him, but I force myself to stay put.

"What are you doing?" I ask him and he looks away from me and back out to the parking lot.

I sigh, disappointment threatening to crush me. I know what he's about to do. I've only known this man for a week now and know he's about to run.

"What was that for?" He asks.

"What?"

"The sigh."

"I'm just so tired of this," I tell him, motioning between the two of us.

He swallows, shifting on his feet, and I decide I have nothing to lose. Might as well lay it all out.

"You look at me like you want me; you even told me you wanted to kiss me since we first met, but then... you're just always running away from me. It's getting really, really old."

He's silent, and I feel so tired all of a sudden. I just want to go inside and go to bed, but I need to get this all out.

"I don't want to play those types of games. I want someone who wants me and isn't afraid to show that. So, until you figure out what it is that you want, I think we should just stay away from each other."

"Lila," he starts, but it's too late for me.

"You've been avoiding me all week. Just go back to that," I tell him as I dig my keys out of my purse and unlock my apartment door.

I don't look back as I head into my apartment and lock the door after me. It hurts to walk away from him, but I know it will probably save me pain in the long run.

I leave the lights off and walk to my room in the dark,

kicking off my shoes and tossing my purse on the couch as I go. I head into my bedroom, plugging my phone in, and that's when I see the messages from Pia.

PIA: **Any updates?**
 Pia: Was he waiting for you in the parking lot?
 Pia: He was, wasn't he??
 Pia: I need details!!

I WISH that I had a better update for her. I know that she'll keep texting me so I respond now.

LILA: **He was waiting for me in the parking lot.**
 Pia: EEK!
 Pia: Then what happened?
 Lila: We kissed.
 Pia: YES! How was it?
 Lila: Amazing. Like I had tingles.
 Pia: Then what happened??
 Lila: Then I told him I was out with you and not on a date, and he pulled back.
 Pia: What an idiot.
 Lila: I told him that we should just stay away from each other until he figures out what it is that he wants.
 Pia: Good for you. You deserve someone who is all in with you. You'll find it.

Lila: I hope
Lila: Good Night.
Pia: Night. Talk to you tomorrow.

I PLUG my phone in and get ready for bed. When I finally crawl between the sheets, all I can think about is that kiss. My fingers trace over my lips, and I can't help but wonder if that will be our one and only kiss as I try to fall asleep.

SEVEN

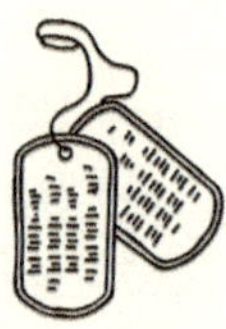

Warren

"HOW ARE THINGS ON BASE?" Gates asks me as he leans back in his chair.

"It's fine," I say distractedly.

I've been distracted for the last four days. Ever since Lila told me that we should just stay away from each other.

I tried to lose myself in work, but that didn't work. All I can think about is Lila. I keep wondering what she's doing and if she's being safe. I've been staying up every night to make sure that she's home and no one is lurking around our apartment building. She even follows me into my dreams, and I wake up wishing that we were really tangled up in bed together.

When work didn't work, I decided to change tactics. So, I called my friends and asked if they wanted to catch up over dinner. I'm hoping that hanging out with the guys helps keep my mind off of my curvy neighbor.

So far, it hasn't worked.

"How's the apartment working out?" Kye asks me.

"It's fine."

The guys share a look and I know that I'm not being very social. I invited them out, and I've been staring off into space for most of the dinner.

"Sorry, I've just been distracted."

"With your neighbor?" Rhett guesses, and I blink.

"Yeah, how did you know that?"

"We have eyes," Gate deadpans.

"Yeah, we all saw you drooling over her when you moved in. I figured you had been spending more time over at her place than your new one," Anson quips.

"I wish," I mumble.

"She's not into you?" Rhett asks.

"She is," I tell them, and they frown.

"Then what's the problem?"

"I don't want to..." I trail off.

"Be with her?" Anson finishes, and I shake my head.

"No, I want to be with her. I don't want to be here. I don't want to put down any roots here when I'm trying my hardest to leave and go back to active duty."

"Okay, well, what do you want more?" Gates asks. "To leave or to be with your little neighbor?"

Lila.

The answer is there as soon as he finishes the question. I want Lila. I want her more than anything. That's why I can't stop thinking about her. It's why I've been miserable since she walked away from me the other night. It's why I haven't been fixated on hating this place so much since I moved in. I need her.

And she needs me too, I think as I remember the man

who was prowling around the parking lot. I haven't seen him since, but I read that there have been a lot of break ins and muggings in our area. I'm guessing that he was looking for an easy score and I scared him off. Still, he could come back, or someone else could target her. *She needs me to protect her and look out for her.*

"Her."

"Then what the hell are you doing?" Gates asks, and I huff out a laugh.

"I have no freaking idea," I admit.

"It's alright. We didn't either, but it worked out fine for us," Rhett says with an easy smile.

All of my friends are happily married and settled down. Some even have kids. I never thought that I would want that, but I do. I want it all with Lila.

Talking to my friends has made me feel better, but I still know that it's going to be an uphill battle to get Lila to forgive me and give me another chance.

"I need to go," I tell them.

"No shit," Rhett mumbles, and I flip him off as I reach for my wallet.

I drop a few twenties on the table and wave as I take off for the door.

"Thanks for dinner!" Anson calls as I leave, and I smile, shaking my head as I jog over to my truck.

The drive home takes forever, and I practice what I want to say to Lila as I go. My speech isn't great, but it's from the heart, and I just hope she's willing to forgive me for being an idiot and give me another chance. I don't know what I'll do if she turns me down.

I park in the lot next to her car and take the stairs two at a time up to her apartment door. I knock, sending up a silent prayer that things go my way as I wait for her to answer the door.

She pulls the door open, looking stoic, and I wish that she would smile. I miss my sunshine and I hate what I've done to her, to both of us.

"I'm an idiot," I blurt out, and her eyebrows rise.

"I'm aware."

"I've been fighting this thing between us, but I can't fight it anymore. I don't want to. I want you. I'm sorry for pushing you away. Please, give me another chance and I'll show you that I'm all in," I promise her.

"Prove it," she challenges.

I take a step towards her, intending to kiss her like I've been dreaming about, but she stops me, placing her hand on my chest.

"Whoa! Not like that," she says, rolling her pretty blue eyes.

"How?"

"Figure it out, Warren," she snaps impatiently.

I know that I deserve that. I never thought I would be bad at dating, but man, I'm a disaster.

She goes to close the door, and my hand shoots out to stop it.

"Have dinner with me tomorrow night."

She studies me, and I pray that she doesn't turn me down.

"I'm tired of running from you and this thing between us," I tell her truthfully. "Have dinner with me and let's see what this thing is between us."

She's still silent, and I'm about to drop down to my knees and beg her to let me take her out tomorrow when she finally puts me out of my misery.

"Fine. Seven o'clock. I'll even let you pick me up."

I smile, relief crashing over me like a wave, and she smiles back slightly.

Then she closes the door in my face.

I sigh, but not in annoyance. I got my second chance, so I can't be mad.

Now, I just need to make sure that I don't mess it up again.

EIGHT

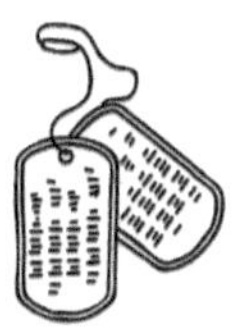

Lila

I'M WEARING the only other dress that I own. My hair is perfectly styled and blown out. I'm prepared to keep my walls up until he's proven that he's not going to run away again. I'm as ready for this date as I can be.

PIA: **Is he there yet?**
   Lila: No, not yet. Any minute though!
   Pia: Have fun! And don't be afraid to make him work for it.
   Lila: Will do. Talk to you later!

PIA SENDS ME A KISS EMOJI, and I smile as I tuck my phone into my purse and check my reflection once again.

A knock comes at the front door and I take a deep breath as I go to answer it. Warren is standing there, his dark brown hair is combed back off of his forehead and he's wearing a black button up shirt and a pair of dark wash jeans. I'm glad to see that I'm not the only one who dressed up a bit.

"Did you check the peephole?" He asks me as I swing the door open and I frown.

"It's seven. Who else could it be? No one else just shows up here."

"Still, you should have checked."

"Is this how you want to start our date?" I ask him, and he scowls.

"I want you to be safe."

"Fine. I'll check from now on," I promise him.

He nods, and I roll my eyes and step out of the apartment, locking the door behind me.

"Where are we going?" I ask him.

"I thought that we would go out to dinner. I made reservations at a few places."

"A few places?" I ask in surprise.

"Yeah, I wasn't sure what you liked and I wanted you to have options."

"Why didn't you just text me and ask?"

"I didn't think of that," he says slowly, and I try to hide my smile as he opens the door of his truck for me and helps me up into the passenger side.

"Well, I'm not picky. I'm good with whatever."

He seems to relax a bit at that. It was cute seeing him so nervous about our date. I like that he's taking this seriously. I love that he's not running from me and this connection between us anymore.

I don't know what it is about Warren, but I've felt so at

ease with him from the beginning. Normally I'm awkward and uncomfortable around new people, especially men, but not with Warren.

I've never had such a strong reaction to anyone before. From that very first moment that we met, he's been all that I can think about. I crave being around him, being with him. I can feel it deep in my bones that what is between us is real and that we're meant to be together. It sounds like he can feel it too. Now I just need to figure out what has been holding him back.

"Seafood sound okay?" He asks as he backs out of his spot and pulls out of the parking lot.

"Sure."

We head towards the coast, and I turn in my seat to face him fully.

"Tell me about yourself," I say, and he frowns.

"What do you want to know?"

"Everything. Anything. All that I really know about you is that your name is Warren, you're a Navy SEAL who is here in California to teach at Coronado, and that you like pepperoni pizza."

"That seems like a lot," he says with a laugh, and I shake my head.

"That's barely anything!" I argue, and he nods.

"Okay, okay. Hmm, let's see. I'm an only child. My dad was in the Army, so we moved around a lot when I was growing up."

"Where have you lived then?"

"All over. South Carolina, Texas, Mississippi, Texas again, Georgia, and then Virginia."

"What about your time in the Navy?"

"I was stationed in Florida, South Carolina, and Washington DC. Oh, and now California."

"Okay, and out of those states, which was your favorite and why?"

"I liked Virginia. The weather was nice and there was a lot to do there."

"Do you like the beach? Or would you rather be in the woods?"

"Beach."

"Figures. You're a SEAL. You must love the water and to swim."

"Yeah, that's why I picked them."

"Was it a hard choice? Picking the Navy?" I ask him as he pulls into the parking lot of Myron's Seafood.

"Not really. I knew that I didn't want to be in the Army, and the others didn't really interest me."

I want to ask him why he didn't want to follow in his father's footsteps but he's already parked and climbing out of the truck. I grab my purse and reach for the door handle, but Warren is already there and opening the door for me.

"Thanks," I say as he offers me his hand and helps me out of the truck.

"Of course. You look beautiful. Did I tell you that yet?"

"No, not yet."

"I should have. You always look gorgeous, though."

"Thanks. You look handsome tonight, too."

We head inside and I let Warren talk to the hostess as I look around the place. I've never been here before. It's always been a little out of my price range. Okay, maybe a lot out of my price range.

"Right this way," the hostess says, and we follow her to the back of the restaurant.

Warren pulls my chair out for me, and I smile at him as I take a seat. He sits across from me, and the hostess hands each of us a menu.

"Your waiter will be right with you."

I nod, and Warren and I take a moment to look over the menu. I haven't had a lot of seafood over the years, mainly because I could never afford it.

"What about you?" Warren asks once he sets his menu aside.

"What about me?"

"Where have you lived?"

"Just California."

"What about trips?"

"No, we never had time for that," I admit.

"Where would you go if price wasn't an option?"

"Anywhere. Everywhere," I tell him with a laugh. "There's so many places that I'd like to see."

"What's stopping you?"

"Money. I, um, I had cancer, and all of our money was going towards treatment."

He stiffens, and I do too. I hate having this talk. I hate telling anyone about me having cancer. They all react the exact same way.

First, they're in shock that someone so young could have been so sick. Then they all give me the same pitying look.

"I had surgery a few months ago, and it's all gone. I'm in remission now," I rush to assure him, and his jaw loosens.

"Good. Fuck, Lila, that must have been so hard. I'm sorry that you had to go through that."

"Me too," I say softly. "It's over now, though. I just have to go in for checkups a little more frequently than most people."

"I love how positive you always are, sunshine."

"I love it when you call me sunshine," I admit, and we share a smile.

"Welcome to Myron's. Can I get you two started with something to drink?"

I let Warren order us some wine, and then we both order our entrees. I get the salmon because I've had that before once and remember liking it. Warren orders the surf and turf, and then the waiter leaves us alone once again.

"Did you have a big family?" I ask him, wanting to steer us to happier topics.

"No. You?"

"No, It was just my parents and Pia. Though I always say that Pia and I are like sisters and that she's all that I ever needed."

"That's your best friend?" He guesses, and I nod.

"Yeah, we've been inseparable forever."

"That must have been nice to have a lifelong friend like that."

"Yeah, I don't know how I would have gotten through life without her."

"What about your parents?" He asks, and my smile drops.

"They were... not the best."

He sits up straighter in his chair, and I force a smile to my lips.

"I had Pia, and her parents were awesome. They took me in, but they passed away a few years ago."

"I'm sorry, Lila."

"It's okay. I still have Pia."

The waiter comes back with our wine and water for each of us.

"What about you?" I ask him.

"My parents?" He asks, and I nod. "They're terrible."

He says it so stoically, so deadpan, and I stare at him in shock.

"What?" I croak out.

"They're terrible parents and terrible people. I can't remember one good memory of them."

"Warren, I'm sorry."

"We seem to be saying that a lot to each other," he remarks, and I smile slightly.

"Way more than I thought I would on my first date," I joke.

"This is your first date?" He asks, and I can feel myself start to blush.

"Yeah, I never really had anyone I was interested in before. I wasn't getting out much with the cancer and all either," I add self-consciously.

"I've never dated before either," he admits, and my mouth drops open.

"What? How is that possible?"

Now it's his turn to blush.

"I was too busy trying to get out of my parents' house, and then I was in boot camp, then here at Coronado to train to become a SEAL. Then I was deploying. It didn't leave a lot of time for dating. Besides, I never met anyone that interested me before."

My body warms at that comment, and I smile as I grab my glass of wine and take a sip.

"What made you want to be a SEAL?"

"I wanted to prove that I was strong and capable and that I was good enough," he says.

As soon as the words are out of his mouth, he looks surprised that he admitted that.

"You are all of those things," I tell him. "And I'm sure you were before you were a SEAL too."

Our waiter comes back with our food and Warren and I

both dig in. We move on to lighter topics, like our favorite seasons, colors, and foods.

The meal goes by far too fast for my liking, and soon he's paying the bill, and we're heading out to his truck.

He takes my hand as he leads me over to his truck and opens the door for me.

"Thanks," I say as he helps me into the passenger seat.

He shuts my door, and I smile as we make the drive back to our apartment building.

"So, how did I do?" Warren asks as we park in the apartment lot.

"Pretty good."

"Am I forgiven?" He asks with a hopeful smile, and I nod.

"Yeah, you're forgiven. I'm not much for grudges anyway."

"Want to do this again? Maybe tomorrow night?"

"Alright," I say, trying to hide my smile.

"Good."

He hops out of the truck, and I gather my things as he opens my door and offers me his hand. He keeps hold of my fingers as we head up to our apartments. We stop outside of my door and I turn to smile up at him.

"I'll see you tomorrow," I say, and he nods, looking hopeful and happy.

"I'll see you then," he says quietly as his head dips towards me.

I lick my lips, my hands resting on his chest as I offer my mouth to him for a kiss.

His lips land on mine and I melt against him, letting him take control as his mouth moves over mine. His lips are so firm yet supple, and I moan as his tongue licks against the seam of my lips.

I open for him, greedy for a taste of him. His tongue tangles with mine, and my hands cling to his shirt as I'm swept away by his kiss. His hands land on my hips and he pulls me flush against him. I moan as I feel his hard cock press against my stomach.

Heat flows through me at the contact, and I find myself wanting to climb him like a tree.

"Excuse me," a man says behind me, and I jump, squeaking as I pull away from Warren and back into my apartment door.

The man passes us and I look up at Warren. We both start laughing at the same time and I smile.

"I'll see you tomorrow."

"Tomorrow," he agrees. "Sleep tight."

"Sweet dreams," I say as I unlock my door and wave goodbye to Warren.

I smile as I lock the door behind me and head towards my room. Now I just need to cool off a bit so that I can fall asleep soon.

Somehow I don't think that that's going to happen.

NINE

Warren

I'M RUNNING LATE and cursing the Los Angeles traffic as I finally pull into the apartment parking lot and throw my truck into park. I climb out and race up the stairs and into my place. I'm supposed to pick Lila up for our second date in twenty minutes, and I'm not about to mess things up by being late.

I know that Lila said she forgave me last night, but I need to make sure that I stay on her good side. I'm not going to blow things with her.

I take the fastest shower of my life, pull on a clean shirt and jeans, then stuff my feet into my socks and shoes and race out the door. Luckily, my girl lives right next door and the commute is quick.

I knock on Lila's door right at seven o'clock and she answers a moment later.

"Hey, sunshine. You look beautiful," I tell her, leaning down to brush a kiss against her cheek.

"Thanks. You don't look so bad yourself," she says with a bright smile.

She grabs her purse and closes the door after herself. I wait for her to lock it before I take her hand and we head downstairs and over to my truck.

"How was work?"

"It was good. We ran late a little bit," I tell her, and she laughs.

"I know. I saw your mad dash upstairs," she admits, and I grin.

"Lucky for me, I can get ready fast."

"Where are we going tonight?" She asks, and I open the door for her.

"I thought we could grab some dinner and then maybe catch a movie. Or take a walk on the beach?"

"Sounds good."

"Anything that you're hungry for?" I ask as I climb behind the wheel.

"I'm not too hungry. Maybe just a sandwich place or something?"

"Sure. I know a deli nearby."

"Perfect."

We take off towards Clark's Deli. It's close to the beach with the biggest and best sandwiches I've ever had. I went there for lunch with some of the guys on one of my first days of work.

"I've never been here," Lila says as we pull into the parking lot.

"It's good."

"What do you usually get?"

"A club sandwich."

"Ohh, that sounds good. I'll get that too."

I smile as I hop out and round the hood to open her

door. I take her hand in mine and we head into the deli. I head up to the counter and order for the both of us. Lila heads to grab us a booth, and I grab our sandwiches and bags of chips and head to join her.

"How was your day?" I ask.

"Good. Busy," she says, popping a Dorito in her mouth. "I got a new client, so I was working on their stuff all day."

"It's cool that you get to pick your own schedule and work from home."

"Yeah, I like it. Sometimes I miss socializing, but then I remember the traffic here and I get over that pretty quickly," she says with a laugh.

We each take a bite of our sandwiches, and she smiles at me.

"This place is really good!"

"I know. Plus, it's huge."

"What did you do today?" She asks me.

"I was doing a test in the pool."

"What kind of test?"

"We bind the candidate's hands and feet, and then they have to sink to the bottom of the pool and push off to go back to the top."

"Whoa, that sounds tough."

"It can be. You just have to stay calm and steady your breathing."

"You've done it before."

"Yeah, I did all of the same tests and training when I was in BUDs."

"I don't think that I could pass," she admits, and I smile.

"You seem like you're stronger than most people realize."

She gives me a pleased smile, and it feels like I'm ten

feet tall. I want to make her look at me like that every single day.

We finish our sandwiches and Lila tells me a bit more about her new client and the work that she does as we drive over to the beach. I park and we look out at the dark coast-line. The wind is whipping sand around as waves crash down hard on the beach.

"Still want to go for a walk?" I ask her and she shivers.

"No, that's okay."

"Did you want to try to catch a movie?" I ask, pulling out my phone to check times.

"Maybe another time. Let's head home," she says and I nod, backing out of my spot and heading off back to our apartment building.

I park in the spot next to her car and hurry to open her door for her and help her out. We hold hands as we head up to her apartment door, and my heart starts to race in my chest as I wonder if she's going to let me kiss her again.

I really hope she does. I've been dreaming about it all day and night.

We both stop outside her door and I hold my breath as she turns to face me.

TEN

Lila

"DO you want to come in for a little bit?" I ask him, and he nods right away.

"Yeah, that would be good."

I unlock the door and we head inside. I swallow hard as I turn to him. I should have asked Pia for some tips on how to do this.

"What are you thinking?" Warren asks me as he closes the door behind us.

"I was trying to figure out how to seduce you," I tell him honestly.

"Just stand there looking at me like that. You're doing great."

"Really?" I ask him, and he nods.

"Yeah. You're gorgeous. How could I not want you?"

No one has ever called me gorgeous before. No one has ever really given me a second thought.

"What do I do now?" I ask him, taking a step closer to him.

"To seduce me?" He asks, and I nod.

"Um, well, you could... kiss me."

He sounds just as clueless about all of this as I am, and I wonder if maybe he's a virgin too.

"Have you never... done this before?" I ask him, and a faint pink stains his cheeks.

"No," he admits.

That takes some of the pressure off of me and I feel bolder. I step towards him, closing the distance between us and running my hands up his chest.

Warren takes a deep, shuddering breath as his head bows towards me. His lips land on mine and I get lost in him as he kisses me. He starts to take over and I gladly let him take the lead.

"Lila," he whispers against my mouth, and I moan.

"I want you," I moan, and his hold on me tightens.

"Are you sure?" He asks, and I nod, pulling back to stare into his blue eyes.

"Did you want to see my bedroom?" I ask him, and he nods his head.

"Fuck yes."

I giggle, taking his hand and leading him down the hallway and into my bedroom.

"It's nice. Bright and welcoming," he says as he looks around the small room.

"Thanks."

He steps towards me, and I reach for the hem of my shirt and pull it over my head. I toss the fabric on my dresser and then take a deep breath before I turn to look at Warren.

His reaction is... not what I expected.

His eyes are dark and hungry as they look over my body.

I've never been naked, or half naked, in front of anyone but Pia. I know that I'm curvy and not everyone's fantasy, but I sure do seem to be Warren's.

"Fuck, sunshine. You look..." he trails off, seemingly at a loss for words.

"Good?" I ask, and he nods.

"Perfect," he corrects, and I smile, feeling more confident. "Your turn."

He nods, reaching behind his neck and pulling his shirt off. All of his muscles are on display now and my mouth waters at the sight.

"Wow. I haven't seen anyone with muscles like that outside of magazines," I tell him, and he chuckles.

He steps towards me, and I can't wait to feel his skin against mine. He's warm, hotter than I thought that he would be, and I shiver as his calloused hands run over my skin. He bows his head and his lips meet mine. His lips are so soft but firm as they move against mine.

He slips his hands into my hair, and I moan as his fingers tug at the strands. I press against him and goosebumps break out all over me.

"Warren," I moan against his mouth, and his fingers tighten in my hair.

He kisses me until I'm breathless and my lips are swollen. When I blink my eyes open, he's watching me, his eyes filled with lust.

"Lila," he croaks, and I nod, my hands reaching for the button on his jeans.

I flick open the button and then tug the zipper down. Warren kicks his shoes off, and we both seem to hold our breaths as I push down his jeans and then he's standing there in his boxers.

"Your turn," he says, and I swallow hard as I reach for my own jeans and undo them.

I push them down, and then I'm standing in front of Warren in just my bra and panties.

"Goddamn," Warren groans, and I blush.

Feeling emboldened, I reach behind me for the clasp of my bra and unhook it. As I pull the straps down my arms, Warren's hands tighten into fists.

"Touch me," I beg him as I drop the bra to the floor.

He doesn't need to be told twice. He steps towards me, and I back up, hitting the mattress and gasping as I fall backward.

Warren grins as he comes down over me, caging me in with his arms. His lips claim mine, and I wrap my arms around him as I get lost in his kiss.

One of his hands slides up my side and he cups my breast. It fits perfectly in his palm, and I moan as I arch against him. His fingers pluck at my nipples, and I shiver in his hold.

"Don't stop," I beg him.

"Never," he promises.

My head tilts back, and I offer more of myself to him. His lips nibble at my earlobe, and I moan as he tugs it between his teeth.

"Warren," I gasp as he licks a path down his neck.

"Keep saying my name like that. I love it," he tells me, and I nod, my eyes falling to half-mast.

His lips trail over my breasts and he licks one nipple and then the other.

"Oh!" I cry, and he does it again.

My hands start to move over his body and I love feeling all of the muscles under his skin. I lovingly explore his body, my hands moving lower and lower until I reach the waistband of his boxers.

"Take these off," I tell him, and he releases my breast reluctantly, rolls onto his side, and slides his boxers off.

My eyes almost bug out of my head when I see his cock, and I gasp.

"Oh my gosh! No way, no freaking way," I say, sliding to the opposite side of the bed.

"What?" Warren asks, alarmed.

"Your dick!"

"What about it?" He asks, worried now.

"It's huge! It will never fit inside me."

He looks down at it and frowns.

"It's not that big," he argues, and I snort.

"Yes, it is."

"Come here," he says, pulling me back to the center of the bed.

He kisses me again and I relax into his hold. My hands start to explore him again, and I take a deep breath, bracing myself as my fingers wrap around his cock.

He moans, and I give him a few subtle strokes. My fingers barely touch around him and he feels like he's as long as my forearm.

"It's my turn to play with you," he tells me, and I shake my head.

"Still my turn."

I push on his chest and roll him onto his back, then start to kiss my way down his chest and then lower.

I wrap one hand around the base of his cock and take a deep breath as I open my mouth wide and wrap my lips around the tip of his dick.

"Fuck! Lila... Jesus," he moans as I start to bob my head up and down his length... or as much of it as I can take.

My hand moves up and down, stroking the part that I can't fit in my mouth. Warren is moaning, his fingers tangling in my hair as I suck him off.

"Lila, sunshine, I need you," he says, tugging on my hair.

He reaches for me and I look up at him.

"Fuck, when you look at me like that. You have no idea what it does to me."

"My turn," he says as he rolls me over onto my back.

He makes quick work of tugging my panties off and throwing them to the side. His lips trail down my neck and over the swell of one breast. He lavishes attention on the plump mound and sucks one of my nipples into his mouth, biting down gently. When I gasp, he releases my nipple and switches to the other breast, giving it the same attention.

When he starts to move lower, I spread my legs wider in invitation.

"So pretty," he murmurs, his fingers spreading my pussy lips.

"Please," I beg, and he licks his lips before he buries his face in my slick folds.

"Oh!" I shout, my legs clamping down on either side of his head as he licks and nibbles along my folds.

His tongue finds my clit, and I almost shoot off the bed as his tongue rolls over it.

"Warren!" I scream, and he does it again.

He moans, slipping one finger against my opening. When he pushes it in slightly, I gasp, my hips moving restlessly against him.

"So tight," he says against my skin, and I start to shiver.

He adds a second finger, and I moan as it starts to feel good. Really good.

I can feel myself starting to get wetter as I get more and

more turned on. I'm close to coming already, and my eyes screw tight as he sucks my clit into his mouth, his fingers twisting inside of me.

"Warren!" I cry, coming fast and hard.

"Fuck," he grunts, licking up my orgasm, and I pant as I start to come down from my high.

Warren kisses his way up my body, and I wrap my legs around his hips as his cock nudges against my opening.

"So fucking sexy," Warren whispers as he starts to push inside of me.

We both hold our breaths as he sinks inside of me. I can feel when he hits my virginity, and I meet his eyes and nod. He kisses me, one hand finding my breast. He plays with my nipple as he thrusts forward and takes my virginity.

"Oh!" I hiss, sucking in a sharp breath.

"I'm sorry, sunshine. I never want to hurt you."

"It's okay. It's already feeling better."

"I'll go slow," he promises me, and I nod.

My grip on him is tight as he starts to move, but soon it starts to feel good. His fingers are still playing with my nipples, and I moan as he kisses my neck.

"You feel so good," he tells me.

"You feel better," I tell him, and feel him smile against my skin.

He's moving in and out of me in a slow, steady rhythm, letting me get used to his big size. My hips start to move in sync with his, and soon, we're both moaning and moving together in perfect sync.

"Lila, Lila, Lila," he chants, and I nod.

"I'm so close," I pant, and he groans as he reaches between us and finds my clit.

"Warren!" I shout as my orgasm races at me.

I come a second later, and Warren groans out my name right after.

He buries his face in my neck, and we both try to catch our breath together.

"Whoa," I breathe out, and he nods.

He pulls out slowly, and I wince slightly.

"Shit, let me get you something. Tylenol?" He asks, and I point to the bathroom.

"In the cabinet."

He heads to get me some medicine, and I smile as I roll over onto my side and watch him head back my way.

"Here you go, sunshine."

He passes me the pills and my cup of water on the bedside table.

"Thanks."

I swallow the pills, and Warren takes the water back before he crawls into bed beside me.

"You're staying?" I ask him, and he nods.

"Is that okay?"

"Yeah," I say with a smile, and he smiles back as he pulls me into his arms.

I fall asleep that night with a smile on my face.

ELEVEN

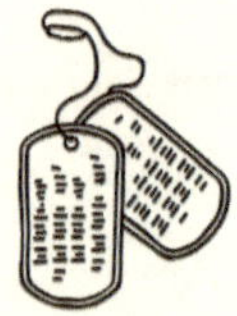

Warren

I NEVER REALLY THOUGHT ABOUT settling down. I guess I assumed that I wouldn't like it. That's why I never looked for a girlfriend and why I never bothered with dating.

Turns out, I love it.

I've been spending all of my free time with Lila. I spend the nights hanging out with her. Sometimes, we watch a movie or cook dinner together. Other times, we go out and then come back and play a board game or watch TV together before I take her to bed and make love to her. Each morning, I wake up in her bed with Lila's curvy frame wrapped around me. I hate to leave her each morning, but I know that in a few short hours, I'll be with her again.

We settled into our new routine quickly, and I had worried that I was moving too fast and that Lila might get sick of me, but she hasn't kicked me out yet.

It's only been a week, but I love it. And I love her too.

I've been trying to figure out the best time to tell her. I've lost count of how many times I've almost said it to her, but none of those times felt perfect. It's getting harder and harder to hold those three words back though.

I wake up with Lila's hair in my face this morning, and smile as I brush the dark strands away and tuck them behind her ear. Her thigh is thrown over my stomach, and she rubs against me slightly. My cock stands at attention at the contact, and I grip her hip.

She blinks her eyes open, smiling up at me, and I lean down, sealing her mouth with mine. She wraps her arms around my neck, and I growl as I kneel between her spread thighs and feel how wet she is for me already.

I break the kiss and start to trail kisses down her neck and over to her tits. She moans, arching against me as I take one stiff nipple into my mouth.

"Warren," Lila moans, squirming underneath me.

Her hands tangle in my hair and she holds me to her as I switch to her other breast. Her hips are restless, moving up and down the length of my cock as I worship her tits.

"Need you," I whisper against the swell of her breast.

"Take me," she begs, her legs opening wider.

I move so that I'm caging her in with my arms and look down at my gorgeous girl. Her cheeks are flushed and her eyes are a dark blue and filled with so much heat that it threatens to burn us both up.

Lila's hands land on my biceps as I start to push into her, and we both hold our breath as I sink in inch by inch.

"So damn tight and perfect," I grit out as I thrust all the way inside of her.

"Oh god," she moans.

I pause to give her time to adjust to my size, and her

hands wrap around my neck. She pulls me down until my lips meet hers.

Her mouth moves against mine in a slow, easy kiss that has tingles racing all over my skin. I get lost in my sunshine and the decadent feel of sliding in and out of her. Her hands are rubbing all over my body, and I love every second of it.

When her hands land on my ass and she pulls me into her more, I get the message and start to move faster, fucking her harder.

"Warren!" Lila shouts as I start to pound into her.

She wraps her legs around my waist, and I grip her thigh, holding her in place as I move in and out of her.

"I... I," I almost tell her I love her, but I bite my tongue and hold the words in.

The middle of sex doesn't feel like the right time to tell her that for the first time.

"Please, Warren," she begs me, and I growl against her neck.

"Fuck, Lila. So tight. So perfect. So *mine*."

Her lips find mine, and I can feel her starting to tighten around me as she starts to reach her peak. I'm not far behind her, and I grit my teeth, holding back my orgasm. I need her to come first.

I pound into her over and over again. Lila is moaning, her nails digging into my arms as she starts to scream.

"WARREN!"

She screams my name as she starts to come all over my cock.

"Fuck, Lila," I groan as I follow right after her.

We're both breathing hard, and I smile as I look into her pretty blue eyes. Her dark hair is mussed and spread out all over the pillows. She's never looked sexier.

"Morning," she says, her voice husky.

"Morning, sunshine."

"Why are we up so early?" She asks. "Not that I'm complaining."

"I have to get to work soon."

She pouts, and I laugh as I pull out of her.

"I know. I hate to leave you, but if I don't shower and get dressed soon, I'm going to be late."

I kiss Lila one last time before I leave her to fall back asleep and crawl out of her bed. I head into the bathroom and then move around, pulling my clothes from last night on to make the trip next door to my own place. When I turn to say goodbye to Lila, she's sound asleep. I grin as I lean down and kiss her forehead.

"See you tonight, sunshine," I whisper against her hair, and she smiles in her sleep.

I smile the whole drive to the base and toss my things down on my desk. I'm about to take a seat and look over the schedule for today when my Commander walks by and calls my name.

"Matthews! I need a word."

"Yes, sir."

I stand and follow him into his office, closing the door behind me. My commander takes a seat and I stand at attention until he motions for me to sit across from him.

"Are you enjoying your time at Coronado, son?" He asks me, and I frown slightly.

"Yes, sir."

He grunts and shuffles some papers on his desk.

"Listen, son. It's no secret that you didn't want this assignment. I'm aware that you tried to get out of it, but the truth is that you're damn good at it. I know that the men you're teaching will be prepared to go out in the field."

"Thank you, sir," I say sincerely.

I didn't think that I would like teaching. It felt like I was being sidelined, but this group has a lot of good guys in it, and I feel like I am making a difference. I am helping them and my country, and that's a good feeling.

"With that being said, a new assignment came up yesterday. So you have a choice. You can continue teaching here, or you can go back to active duty."

"What?" I croak.

"You heard me. You have three days to decide. I need your decision by Friday morning," he tells me, and I nod.

He nods to the door, and I know that I've been dismissed.

I leave in a daze and head back to my desk, collapsing into my chair.

"Shit," I mumble.

A few weeks ago, this would have been a dream come true. I thought that being on active duty and being deployed was what I wanted for my life. Now that I've met Lila and been at Coronado, though, I'm having second thoughts.

What the heck do I do now?

TWELVE

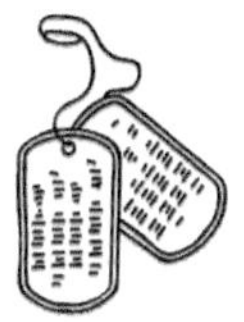

Lila

WORRY HAS BEEN NAGGING at me all day. Warren is starting to act weird. He's been silent all day, even more so than usual, and I'm worried that he might be about to pull another disappearing act. Normally, he texts me whenever he can throughout the day, and lets me know when he's leaving, but he hasn't texted me or responded to one of my texts once today.

I'm about to reach my limit. I've decided that when he gets out of the shower, I'm going to confront him and demand that he tell me why he's acting strange and pulling back from me again.

I hear his footsteps heading towards my apartment, and I stop pacing and straighten my shoulders. He knocks, and I make a big show of checking the peephole before I open the door.

"Hey, sunshine," he says distractedly as he heads into the living room.

"Hey, how was work?" I ask as I close the door.

"Fine."

"We need to talk," I sigh, and he whips around to look at me.

"About what?"

"What the heck is going on with you?"

"Nothing."

"Stop lying! You're blocking me out again, and I'm not going through that again."

"Sunshine," he starts, coming towards me, and I shake my head.

"Just tell me what's going on," I demand, and he sighs.

"I was told that I can go back to active duty. I could be back on the East Coast in a few weeks."

My stomach and heart both drop. My knees threaten to give out, too, and I move over to the couch and sit down before that can happen.

"So, you're leaving," I say, my voice sounding emotionless to my own ears.

"I don't know," he says softly.

Tears sting the back of my eyes and I swallow hard.

"I'm going to head back to my place and think for a bit," he says after a few moments, and I nod wordlessly.

He leaves, and I get up and lock the door after him. This is the first time all week that he's gone back to his own apartment, and I'm not taking that as a good sign.

I look at my empty apartment and I know that I can't stay here tonight. I grab my phone and dial Pia's number.

"Hey, Lila! I was just about to call you. How's it going?"

"Bad," I choke out, and she gasps.

"Oh, Lila. Come here. We'll have a girls' night."

"I don't want to impose."

"You're not!" She promises me.

"You're always welcome here!" Levi calls, and I smile slightly.

"Okay, I'll be over soon."

"See you in a bit."

We hang up and I go to pack a bag. Warren still isn't back by the time that I'm packed so I leave without saying goodbye to him and head down to my car.

The drive over to Pia's seems to take forever. When it starts to rain, all I can think is that it seems fitting.

Pia is waiting for me in the lobby of her apartment building and she opens her arms for a hug as soon as she spots me heading her way.

"I'm so sorry, Lila," she whispers, and I nod, choking back a sob.

"Me too."

"Let's go upstairs."

I nod again, and she links our arms as we head over to the elevator.

Being here is still strange to me. Lila and I grew up living in rundown apartments. We never even dreamed that we would be able to live in an apartment building like this, and definitely not in the penthouse.

Being here still makes me a bit uncomfortable. I'm always afraid that I'm going to break something that I can't afford. Pia seems to be at home, though, and I'm glad since this is her home now.

We ride up to the top floor in silence. I can feel how worried she is about me, but I don't have the energy to lie and reassure her that I'm alright. The truth is that I'm not okay. It feels like my heart has been broken and all of the jagged pieces are floating around inside of me.

"Do you want to talk about it?" She asks me gently as we step off of the elevator into the penthouse.

"I don't know what to say. Everything was going so perfectly. I was really happy, and I know that he was too. Now that he has this job offer, though, he's going to leave. He won't choose me," I say, and the dam breaks with those words.

I cry, and she pulls me into her arms, hugging me tightly.

"He will, Lila. Anyone would. You're amazing."

"He loves being a SEAL. He loves being out there. He told me so himself. He said that teaching felt like being sidelined."

"Maybe he's changed his mind. I mean, the fact that he didn't immediately take the new assignment has to mean something, right?" She asks, and I sniffle.

"I don't know."

She leads me over to the couch, and I see Levi walk in, take one look at me crying and hurry back out. Seeing his distressed face and how fast he turned around almost has me laughing. Then I remember how Warren left my apartment and my smile drops.

"Want to eat junk food and watch a movie?" Pia asks, and I shrug.

"Sure. I was hoping that I could stay here for a few days. I'm just not ready to see Warren again yet."

"Of course. You're always welcome here, you know that."

"Did someone say chocolate?" Levi asks, walking in carrying a few bags of Lindt chocolate and a container of brownies.

"We didn't, but this is perfect. Thanks, honey," Pia says, and he smiles at her as he sets everything down on the coffee table in front of us.

"I'll leave you two to it. Let me know if you need anything else."

"We will."

"Thanks, Levi," I say weakly, and he gives me a kind smile.

He kisses Pia before he heads back to his office, and I sigh as I grab the brownies.

"So, what are we watching?" Pia asks as she grabs the remote. "Maybe we should order pizza or something. Are you hungry?"

I let her chatter away at me and pick a show for us. I'm trying to pay attention, but it's hard. I find myself staring out at the dark, rain-covered windows and watching the bleary lights of the city blink out one by one.

I wish Warren would pick me, but I know I can't ask him to. I don't want him to regret his choice or resent me later on. If he wants to return to being active duty, I need to let him.

I just wish he had gotten this offer before I went and fell in love with him.

THIRTEEN

Warren

I DON'T KNOW why I didn't just tell my Commander that I wanted to stay the moment he offered me that choice. Since I can't leave Lila, and I know that she doesn't want to leave Los Angeles or California. Not if it means being away from Pia.

I should have told my commander I was staying right then and there. Instead, I messed things up with Lila once again. I know that I hurt her and I hate that. The truth is that I walked into his office the next morning and told him that I wanted to stay.

Now that my job is secure, I need to secure my relationship with Lila. I know that I can't live without Lila. Except now I can't find her to tell her that.

I went back twenty minutes after I left to tell her that I chose her, that I just needed a few quiet moments to wrap my head around it, but that, of course, I was always going to choose her. Except, when I went back to her place, she was gone and she never came back.

She hasn't been home all weekend, and I would know. I've been knocking on her door and checking the parking lot every hour. I've tried calling and texting her, but her phone must be off because it goes straight to voicemail each time.

I'm starting to lose my mind. It's been three days, and I need her. I need to tell her what she means to me.

I know she has to be with Pia, but I don't know her last name or phone number to call and ask to talk to her. So, I've resorted to driving around to her favorite restaurants and spots trying to find her. Anywhere that she's mentioned, I've driven by, but so far, I haven't been able to spot her.

I drag my tired body out to my truck to make the drive home. I don't have much hope that she'll be home tonight, but I can't stop myself from looking for her car in the parking lot and glancing up at her apartment for any lights or signs of movement as I pull into the lot.

When I see her car, I sit up straighter in my seat. I barely park my truck before I'm out and sprinting up the steps and to her door.

I knock, waiting impatiently for her to answer. When she does, my heart lodges in my throat. She looks so pretty, but she doesn't smile up at me.

"Here to tell me that you're an idiot again?" She asks blandly, and I swallow hard.

"I'm here to tell you that I love you. That I choose you. That I'm staying because I don't want to be anywhere you aren't. I need you, sunshine."

She blinks, her mouth dropping open.

"I am an idiot. I've been waiting for the perfect time to tell you, but I should have told you when I first realized how

I felt about you. I shouldn't have let you doubt for one second that I wanted you and would always choose you."

"You told me that you didn't know what you were going to do," she points out and I nod.

"I know. I thought that I still wanted my old life. I was going to ask you to come with me, but I realized I couldn't do that to you. I know that you don't want to leave Pia, and I don't want to ask you to. I don't want to deploy and leave you for months at a time. I don't want to leave you at all."

"Why did it take you so long to realize that?" She asks, crossing her arms over her chest.

"It didn't. It just took me a little bit to let go of what I thought I wanted and wrap my head around everything."

"You should have talked to me, told me what you were thinking. Instead, you just left me here wondering."

"I know. I'm not used to running things by other people, but I swear I will in the future. I need to work on my communication skills, and I promise that I will."

"We're supposed to be partners and you shut me out. Again."

"I'm sorry, Lila. I am an idiot, but I swear, I'm a fast learner. I won't make these mistakes again."

"You hurt me," she says softly, and I hate myself.

"I'm sorry. It's the last thing that I want to do. I just want to make you smile."

She studies me and I try not to fidget.

"I missed you these last few days. I've been by a few times."

"I was with Pia."

"I figured. I tried to call and text you, too."

"I know. I got them when I charged my phone."

"I love you, Lila. I'll do anything for you to believe me

and give me another chance to show you just how much you mean to me."

She sighs, and her arms drop down to her sides.

"I forgive you. I talked to Anson and Rhett. They told me how hard the transition is to go from active duty to civilian and that you were just a little slow to figure out what you wanted."

"You did?"

"Yeah. Pia is friends with Lottie's best friend and they came over for girls' night the other night. Rhett and Anson dropped them off."

"I'll have to send them a gift basket."

"I believe they said you could take them out for a burger and beer."

I huff out a relieved laugh and take a step towards her.

"Do you want me to take you out? We can go to that fusion place you like," I offer.

"I already ate."

I nod, trying not to look too desperate to be around her.

"But you can come in."

"I should probably take a shower," I say, even as I follow her into her apartment. "I've been in the pool for most of the day."

"You can shower here... or we can shower together."

My cock strains against my zipper as an image of Lila, wet and naked, fills my head.

"Yes, let's do that."

She laughs as I take her hand and drag her after me into her apartment. She follows me into her bathroom and reaches for the buttons of my jacket. I help her undo them, and together, we pull each other's clothes off.

"I missed you. I love you," I tell her as I pull her against me and kiss her.

"I missed you too. I love you so much, Warren."

I pepper kisses down her neck and then grab her hips and boost her up onto the bathroom vanity. Lila spreads her legs for me to fit between them, and I smile down at her as I kiss her full lips.

"Let me love you," I whisper against her lips, and she nods.

I kiss her once more, then drop to my knees before her. She gasps as I push her thighs wider apart. Her pussy is slick with need, and I lick my lips as I trail kisses up her thighs. When I reach her core, I lick my lips and then dive in.

I lick her pussy and moan at her flavor.

"Warren! Oh god!" She cries, and I grin as I suck her clit into my mouth and worship the little pearl.

My hands pin her in place so that she can't get away from me and I lick a path from her snug hole back up to her clit.

Lila's legs start to shake, and I know that she's close to coming. She just needs a little... bit... more...

"Warren!" Lila shouts as she comes, and I greedily lick up all of her juices.

I give her one more lick before I push to my feet and step back between her thighs. Lila looks dazed, but she smiles up at me and wraps her arms around my neck as my cock nudges against her dripping-wet opening.

We're both so on edge after being apart for the last few days, and I know that this first time together isn't going to last long.

Lila wraps her legs around my waist, and I grip her hips as I thrust into her in one hard move.

"Oh!" Lila gasps, and I love the sounds she makes.

I start to pound into her, taking her hard and fast.

Already Lila's pussy is strangling my cock, and I know that neither of us will be able to last much longer. I just need to make sure that Lila comes first.

I'm close though. So damn close.

I reach between us and my fingers find her clit and press on that tight bundle of nerves.

"Warren!" She screams, and I hear the neighbors on the other side of us start to bang on the wall, telling us to keep it down.

I dip my head to kiss her, cutting off her cries of pleasure as my tongue slips into her mouth.

As soon as her tongue flicks against mine, I start to come, and I moan against her mouth as I find my own release deep inside of her.

We're both covered in sweat and out of breath as we hold onto each other. I don't want to let her go, so I reach over, turning on the shower before I pick her up and carry her under the spread.

"Again?" Lila asks breathlessly, and I grin.

"Again."

And we do it again, and again, and again.

FOURTEEN

Lila

FIVE YEARS LATER...

I WAKE up with Warren holding me close. He's so hot, and I kick the comforter off of me as I snuggle closer to him.

"Mmm, good morning, sunshine," Warren says in his gravelly morning voice.

"Morning," I whisper back.

He kisses the back of my neck, nuzzling into me, and I giggle as his scruff tickles my sensitive skin.

"We could be quiet," he whispers, his hands sliding up under my pajamas.

"When have I ever been quiet?" I ask with a giggle, and I feel him grin against my skin.

He kisses my neck, and I glance over at the alarm clock, gasping when I see how late it is.

"Warren! It's already seven thirty."

"Shit!" He groans, giving me one more kiss before he climbs out of bed and hurries into the bathroom.

I smile as I get out of bed, too, and pad downstairs and into the kitchen. I start the coffee machine, grab a bagel, and pop it in the toaster. I can hear Warren moving around upstairs, and I manage to grab the cream cheese out of the fridge right as Warren comes downstairs.

I smear cream cheese on the bagel and pass it to Warren as he joins me in the kitchen.

"Thanks, sunshine. I don't know what I would do without you."

He kisses my cheek and I smile as I pour us each a cup of coffee.

"What do you have planned for today?" Warren asks me as he rushes around the kitchen, packing his lunch and getting ready to leave for work.

"Noah and I are going to go over to Pia's place for a play date this morning," I tell him, and he nods.

"Tell Pia and Annie that I said hi."

"I will. Want to grab dinner downtown with them tonight?"

"Sounds like a plan. I'll be home at five," he says, kissing me goodbye before he heads out the door.

I stand at the door and wave as he hops in his truck and backs out of the driveway. Noah, our son, is still asleep upstairs, and I know I have at least another hour before he'll be up. I grab my cup of coffee and head into the living room to enjoy the quiet.

Warren proposed to me a month after he decided to stay in California and continue teaching at Coronado. I, of course, said yes. We had moved in together by then and were spending all of our free time together, and I couldn't wait to spend the rest of my life with him.

We got married in a small ceremony on the beach. I had Pia as my maid of honor, and Warren's SEAL friend, Keaton, was his best man. We had a few of his other SEAL friends in attendance, too. After the ceremony, we went to my favorite steakhouse for dinner, and then Warren and I got on a plane the next day and spent a week in Hawaii for our honeymoon.

We moved into this house a few months later and started talking about growing our family. We were both concerned with any of our kids having a higher risk of having cancer, so we opted to adopt instead.

It took us a year and a half, but then we were able to adopt our Noah. He was nine months old when we adopted him, but he took to us right away. He's always been such a happy, sweet boy, and Warren and I fell in love with him instantly.

We had talked about trying to adopt another child, but I like our little family. The first adoption process was so long and stressful, and I'm not sure that I could go through that again. We both agree that our family feels complete with just the three of us, and I'm happy to just focus on my boys.

I curl up on the couch with my coffee and listen to the quiet of the house. I love having these moments by myself before the craziness of the day.

I'm still working as a freelance social media manager, though I've cut back on my clients so that I can focus on Noah.

Tiny footsteps sound on the floor above me, and I smile as I stand and go to greet my son. I never thought that I would get to say that. I never thought I would have kids, a husband, or a house. Then I met Warren, and everything that I never thought I would have started to happen.

It's been five years, and I've never been happier. I can't wait to see what the next five years have in store for us.

"Mommy!" Noah cheers as he comes downstairs and sees me waiting for him.

"Noah!" I repeat, and he laughs as I pick him up and spin him around.

"Are you ready for our fun day?" I ask him, and he grins at me, nodding his little head. "Are you ready to see Aunt Pia and Annie?"

He nods again, and I smile as I carry him into the kitchen to get both of us ready for our fun day.

My phone buzzes, and I look at it as I set Noah down on his feet.

WARREN: **I forgot to tell you how beautiful you look and how much I love you this morning.**

Lila: I haven't even brushed my hair yet.

Warren: Doesn't matter. You're still the most beautiful woman in any room.

Lila: Awww

Lila: Love you, babe!

Warren: Love you more, sunshine. See you tonight.

I SET my phone aside and smile as I start on breakfast.

Looking for Pia and Levi's story? Check out the complete Billionaire Bosshole series here!

Looking for the Knight Security series? You can read the complete series here!

Looking for more military romance books? Check out A Very Grumpy Valentine's Day, Fallen Peak: Military Heroes, and The Trouble With Needing today!

CONNECT WITH ME!

If you enjoyed this story, please consider leaving a review on Amazon or any other reader site or blog that you like. Don't forget to recommend it to your other reader friends.

If you want to chat with me, please consider joining my VIP list or connecting with me on one of my Social Media platforms. I love talking with each of my readers. Links below!

<u>Website</u>
<u>Newsletter</u>

A Very Mountain Man New Year

<u>Folklore</u>

<u>Kidnapping His Forever</u>

<u>Claiming His Forever</u>

<u>Finding His Forever</u>

<u>Rescuing His Forever</u>

<u>Chasing His Forever</u>

<u>Folklore: The Complete Series</u>

<u>Holiday Hearts</u>

Be Mine

Falling in Love

Holly Jolly Holidays

<u>Love Notes</u>

<u>Signing Off With Love</u>

<u>Care Package Love</u>

<u>Wrong Number, Right Love</u>

<u>Kings Gym</u>

Fighting Fire With Fire

Fighting Tooth and Nail

Fighting Back From Hell

<u>Mine To</u>

<u>Mine to Love</u>

<u>Mine to Protect</u>

<u>Mine to Cherish</u>

<u>Mine to Keep</u>

Mine to: The Complete Series

<u>Sequoia: Stud Farm</u>

Branded

Bucked

Roped

Spurred

<u>Sequoia: Fast Love Racing</u>

Jump Start

Pit Stop

Home Stretch

<u>Telltale Heart</u>

<u>Bought and Paid For</u>

<u>His Miracle</u>

<u>Pretty Girl</u>

<u>Telltale Hearts Boxset</u>

ALSO BY SHAW HART

Still in the mood for Christmas books?

Stuffing Her Stocking, Mistletoe Kisses, Snowed in For Christmas, Coming Down Her Chimney

Love holiday books? Check out these!

For Better or Worse, Riding His Broomstick, Thankful for His FAKE Girlfriend, His New Year Resolution, Hop Stuff, Taming Her Beast, Hungry For Dash, His Firework

Looking for some OTT love stories?

Her Scottish Savior, Baby Mama, Tempted By My Roommate, Blame It On The Rum, Wild Ride, Always

Looking for a celebrity love story?

Bedroom Eyes, Seducing Archer, Finding Their Rhythm

In the mood for some young love books?

Study Dates, His Forever, My Girl

Some other books by Shaw:

The Billionaire's Bet, Her Guardian Angel, Falling Again, Stealing Her, Dreamboat, Making Her His, Trouble